Peppa Goes Camping

Today, Peppa and George are very excited.
They are going on holiday!
Daddy Pig has a surprise. Honk, honk!
"It's a camper van," grunts Daddy Pig.
"Wow!" gasp Peppa and George.

"We're going on holiday!" sings Peppa.
"We're going on holiday, in our camper van! Snort!"
"Hmmm," says Daddy Pig, looking at the map.
"Daddy Pig!" cries Mummy Pig. "Are we lost?"
"Well, er," begins Daddy Pig, "yes!"

Granddad Dog and Danny Dog arrive. "Hello," calls out Peppa. "We're lost!"

"Lost?" asks Granddad Dog, confused. "Is your satnav broken?" Peppa, George, Mummy and Daddy Pig don't know what satnav is.

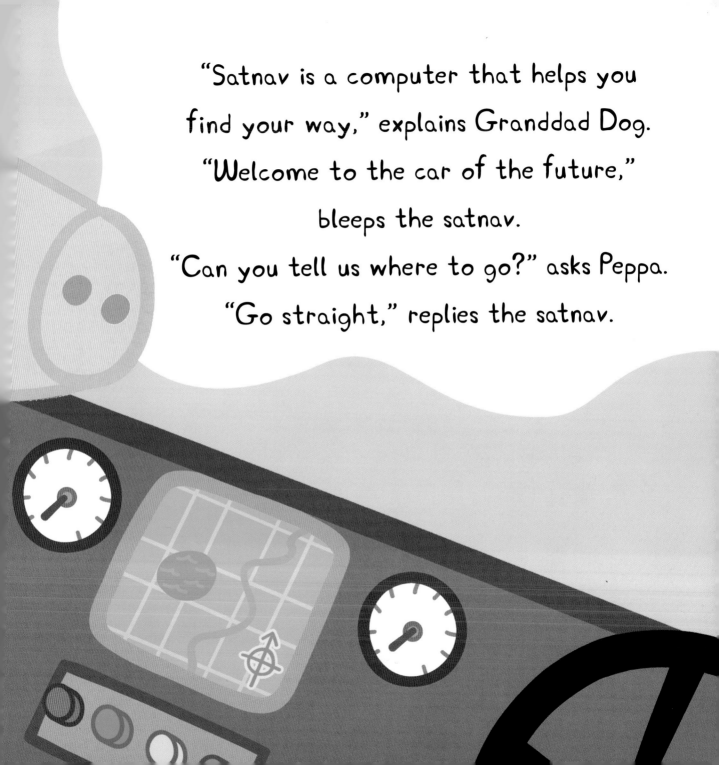

"Satnav is a computer that helps you find your way," explains Granddad Dog. "Welcome to the car of the future," bleeps the satnav. "Can you tell us where to go?" asks Peppa. "Go straight," replies the satnav.

Daddy Pig thanks Granddad Dog
and the family continue on their way.
"We're going on holiday," sings Peppa.
"We're going on holiday, in our camper van!"
Suddenly, the camper van is low on oil.
But Daddy Pig can't find the engine!

Mummy Sheep and Suzy Sheep arrive in their car.
"Hello, Suzy," cries Peppa. "We've lost our engine!"
"Lost your engine?" replies Mummy Sheep.
"I don't know a thing about engines,"
says Mummy Sheep. "But I'll have a look."

"I'm probably wrong, but this looks like an engine,"
says Mummy Sheep, lifting the boot.
"Well spotted, Mummy Sheep," gasps Daddy Pig,
pouring oil into the engine. Glug, glug!
Daddy Pig thanks Mummy Sheep
and the family are off again!

"Are we nearly there yet?" asks Peppa, sighing.

"Just up the next hill," says the satnav.

"You have reached your destination," says the satnav when they get to the top of a steep hill.

"Hooray!" everyone cheers.

"Time for bed," says Mummy Pig.
Peppa and George put on their pyjamas.
"But where will we sleep?" asks Peppa.
"Mummy Pig and I will sleep on this bed,"
says Daddy Pig, pressing a button.
Whirrr!

"Ta-da! A lovely big bed appears in the room.

"And you two will sleep upstairs like
you always do," says Mummy Pig.

"Watch this," says Daddy Pig,
pressing another button.

Whirrr! Click . . .

Suddenly, the camper van's roof lifts up and
a bunk bed appears. Daddy Pig tucks
Peppa and George into bed.
"The camper van is just like our
little house!" says Peppa.
"Goodnight, everyone," says the satnav. "Sleep well!"

Snore!

Snore!

Snore!

Snore!